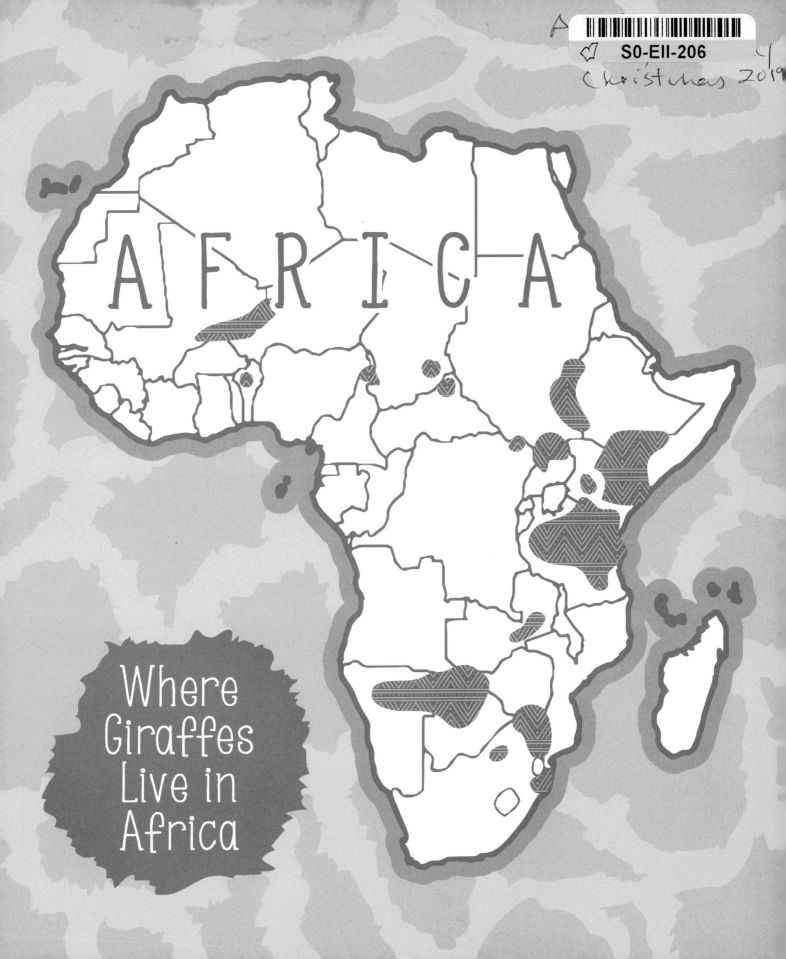

A F R I C A

Christmas 2019

Where
Giraffes
Live in
Africa

Ty

the
Quiet
Giraffe

Carrie Hasler

Illustrated by Barbara Ball

SAN DIEGO ZOO GLOBAL PRESS

At first, everyone noticed Ty the giraffe. It was hard not to. He couldn't help but stand out. Everyone had so many questions for him. But Ty didn't answer. He didn't know quite what to say.

Ty was shy. Ty was a quiet guy.

At school, Ty always paid attention. He liked listening to the teacher, and he never interrupted. Instead, he patiently waited to be called on.

But not everyone was like Ty. Some were always chattering away. Others, like Eric the rhino, couldn't help but blurt out the answers before anyone else had a chance.

I know the answer! I know the answer! It's four!

Is an inchworm really an inch?

When the others were monkeying around in art, Ty was focused. He wanted his drawings to be the best they could be. His notebook was full of sketches and fancy doodles, not messy scribbles.

During story time, Stuart the warthog kept interrupting to tell everyone what would happen next. Even though Ty had already heard the story too, he never gave it away. He kept it to himself.

At the watering hole, Ty could hear Zari the zebra whispering with her friends.

"Ty's so quiet," said Zari. "Why doesn't he ever speak?"
"I don't know. Maybe he can't speak," the elephant replied.
"Ty never has anything to say," snickered the hyena.

They all giggled.

Ty might be quiet, but he could hear quite well. Even though Ty was very tall, he was beginning to feel very small.

But Ty liked being quiet. When he was quiet, he could listen. He could hear the crickets chirping in the evening dusk. He could hear the first raindrops of a storm polka-dot across the earth. He could watch the busy termites repair their mound.

Ty noticed things that no one else did.

The thing Ty loved best of all was being with
his bird friends, the oxpeckers. Because he was
quiet and calm, they would perch on his neck and ride
on his back and play with him among the branches. He loved
watching them build their nests in the crevices and holes of
his favorite acacia tree. They would tell him their stories.
Ty was always the best listener.

No one ever noticed the oxpeckers.
But Ty did.

The next day at recess, Ty looked around for someone to play with. Stuart was too much of a ball hog. The honey badgers were too bossy. Playing dung beetle marbles looked fun, but he felt too shy to ask if he could join. What if they said no?

"Ty's too quiet. He won't be any fun to play with. He never has anything to say," chimed in Zari when it was time to pick teams.

Eventually, everyone stopped noticing Ty.

That afternoon the teacher was asking a lot of questions, like she usually does: "What is the name of a group of lions?" and "What do herbivores eat?"

Ty didn't like raising his hoof right away. He liked to think about his answer before sharing it.

What do you think, Ty?

There was a long pause as Ty was thinking. Everyone was waiting and waiting, but Eric couldn't wait any longer.

He doesn't think ANYthing! Ty's too quiet. He never has anything to say!

Sad and discouraged, Ty trudged home after school. He didn't think being quiet was a bad thing, but maybe it was. He decided to visit his oxpecker friends, knowing they would cheer him up.

When he got to the acacia tree, he soon forgot about his troubles when he noticed that one of the birds—the smallest one—had fallen and broken her wing. There wasn't enough room in the nest.

She just couldn't fit in.

After helping her up, Ty had an idea. He remembered listening to the math lesson, and he thought about the story his teacher read. He pulled out the drawing he had done in art class.

Ty got busy.

Ty didn't care that the others at school thought he was too quiet. He had important work to do. Ty began measuring and sawing, hammering and painting. Day after day, he rushed home, excited to work on his project.

One afternoon while everyone was playing, Ty looked out across the savanna, thinking about his oxpecker friends. He was as tall as a watchtower and could see far into the distance.

Suddenly, his ears began to twitch, and the hair along his neck began to stand up. Ty could see a threatening cloud of sand and dust billow along the horizon. The ground began to rumble with the sound of 10,000 hoofs.

Like scissors cutting through the air, Ty's long legs carried him back to the playground to warn the others.

"STAMPEDE!"

shouted Ty with all his might.

Surprised to hear his
voice, the others turned and
raced, following Ty across the
grass to the protection of the
umbrella-shaped acacia tree just
as the first of the wildebeests
stormed past.

Huddled behind the tree trunk, the
animals hunkered down as the herd
parted and the dust and the dirt settled.

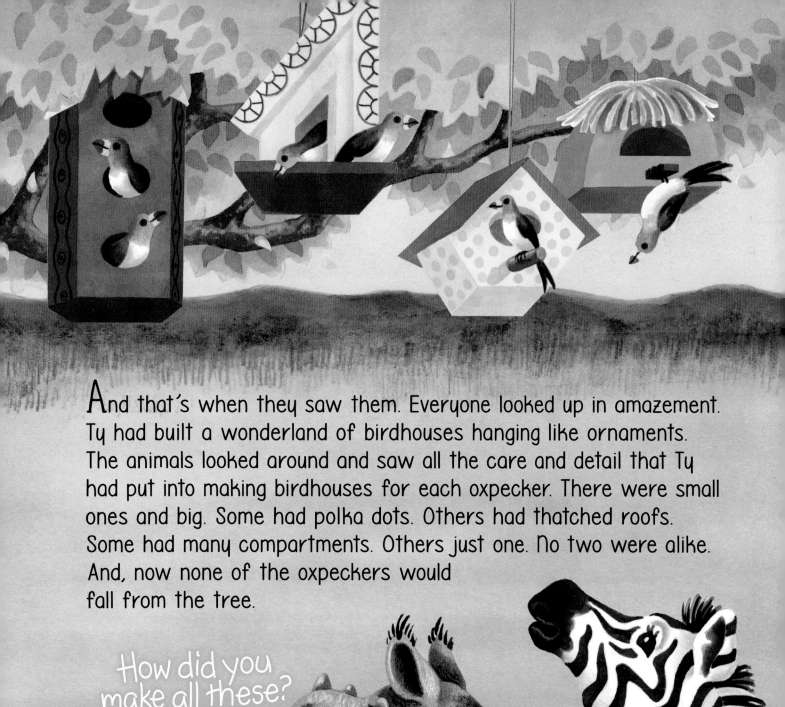

And that's when they saw them. Everyone looked up in amazement.
Ty had built a wonderland of birdhouses hanging like ornaments.
The animals looked around and saw all the care and detail that Ty
had put into making birdhouses for each oxpecker. There were small
ones and big. Some had polka dots. Others had thatched roofs.
Some had many compartments. Others just one. No two were alike.
And, now none of the oxpeckers would
fall from the tree.

How did you make all these?

All
friends
welcome

Then they all noticed the sign.

Everyone looked at each other and up to the birdhouses and then back at the sign. And, like the grass rippling across the savanna, the animals realized what Ty had shown them. There is room for everyone.

Will you show me how to make a birdhouse?

They all looked up at Ty. He was hard not to notice. In fact, he seemed taller than before.

It turns out, Ty might be quiet, but he has a lot to say.

For Cate,
*my favorite quiet person who
has so much to say.* —CH

For Steve,
*my greatest encourager and
most helpful critic.* —BB

Ty the Quiet Giraffe was published by San Diego Zoo Global Press in
association with Blue Sneaker Press. Through these publishing efforts, we seek to
inspire multiple generations to care about wildlife, the natural world, and conservation.

San Diego Zoo Global is committed to leading the fight against extinction.
It saves species worldwide by uniting its expertise in animal care and conservation
science with its dedication to inspire a passion for nature.

Douglas G. Myers, President and Chief Executive Officer
Shawn Dixon, Chief Operating Officer
Yvonne Miles, Corporate Director of Retail
Georgeanne Irvine, Director of Corporate Publishing
San Diego Zoo Global
P.O. Box 120551
San Diego, CA 92112-0551
sandiegozoo.org | 619-231-1515

Blue Sneaker Press works with authors, illustrators, nonprofit organizations,
and corporations to publish children's books that engage, entertain,
and educate kids on subjects that affect our world.
Blue Sneaker Press is an imprint of Southwestern Publishing Group, Inc.,
2451 Atrium Way, Nashville, TN 37214. Southwestern Publishing Group
is a member of Southwestern Family of Companies.

Southwestern Publishing Group, Inc.
swpublishinggroup.com | 800-358-0560

Christopher G. Capen, President
Kristin Connelly, Managing Editor
Lori Sandstrom, Art Director

Text and illustrations copyright ©2019 San Diego Zoo Global

ISBN: 978-1-943198-08-5
Printed in the Republic of Korea (ROK)

Library of Congress Control Number: 2019937389
10 9 8 7 6 5 4 3 2 1

More Fun Facts!

Giraffes are sometimes called the "watchtowers" of the savanna, because they are so tall and are often the first to notice approaching danger.

Elephants flap their large ears to cool themselves off.

A group of rhinos is called a crash.

To get a drink of water, giraffes have to splay their legs or kneel down.

Giraffes live in groups called herds.

The honey badger is known as a fierce and aggressive fighter. With sharp claws, strong teeth, and an awful odor, a honey badger is not an animal to mess with!

African termites can build mounds that are 17 feet tall.

A giraffe's long neck and long tongue help it reach leaves high up in the trees.

African elephants have large ears that are shaped like the continent of Africa.

Herbivores are animals that only eat plants.